ARCHIE

LOVES SKIPPING

FOR

A·F
+
J·F

Bloomsbury Publishing, London, New Delhi, New York and Sydney

First published in Great Britain in 2015 by Bloomsbury Publishing Plc
50 Bedford Square, London, WC1B 3DP

A CIP catalogue record for this book is available from the British Library

ISBN 978 1 4088 2930 1

1 3 5 7 9 10 8 6 4 2

Printed in China by C & C Offset Printing Co Ltd, Shenzhen, Guangdong

All papers used by Bloomsbury Publishing are natural, recyclable products
made from wood grown in well-managed forests. The manufacturing processes
conform to the environmental regulations of the country of origin

www.bloomsbury.com
www.domenicamoregordon.com

BLOOMSBURY is a registered trademark
of Bloomsbury Publishing Plc

ARCHIE

LOVES SKIPPING

Domenica More Gordon

BLOOMSBURY

LONDON NEW DELHI NEW YORK SYDNEY

Tra la la . . .

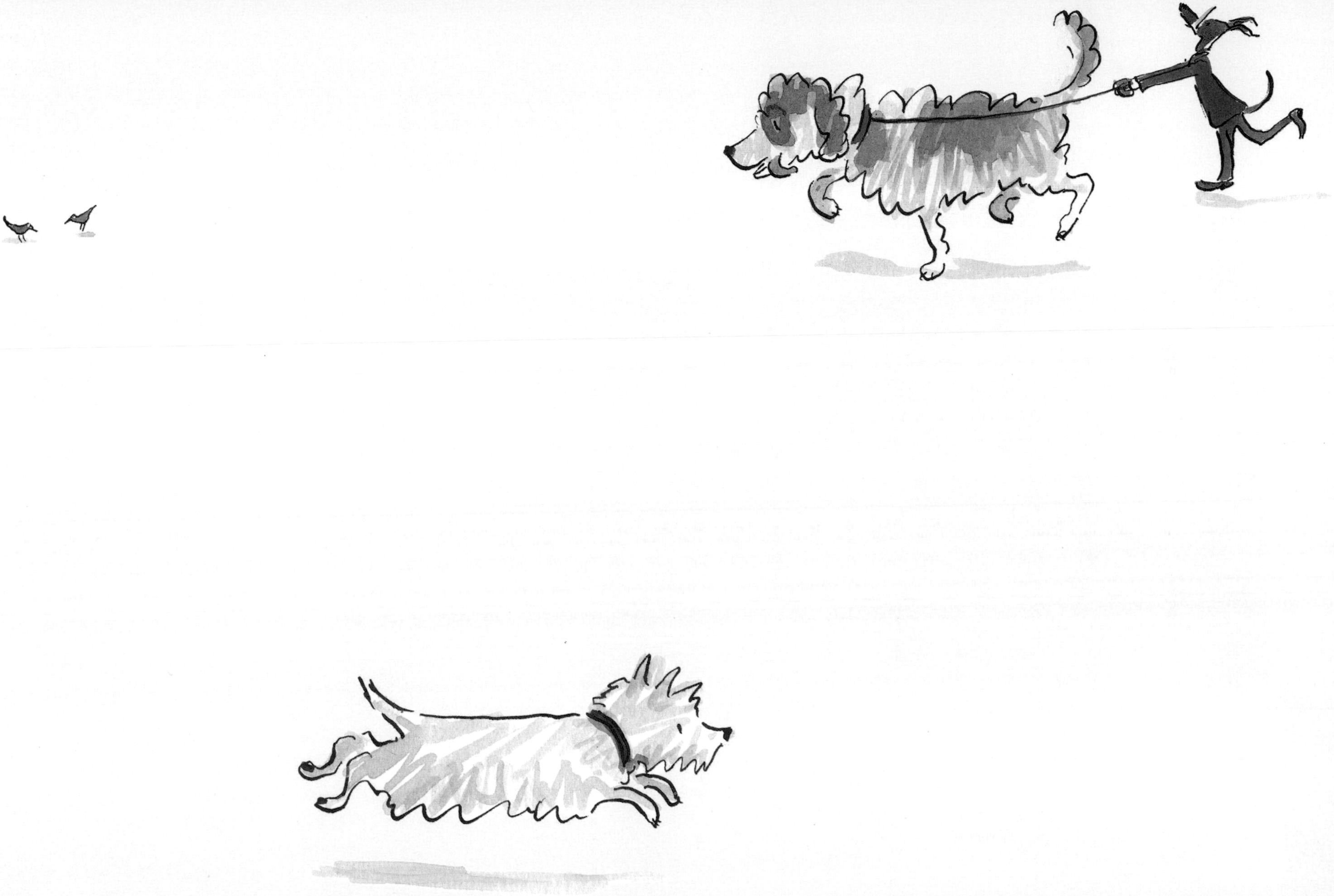

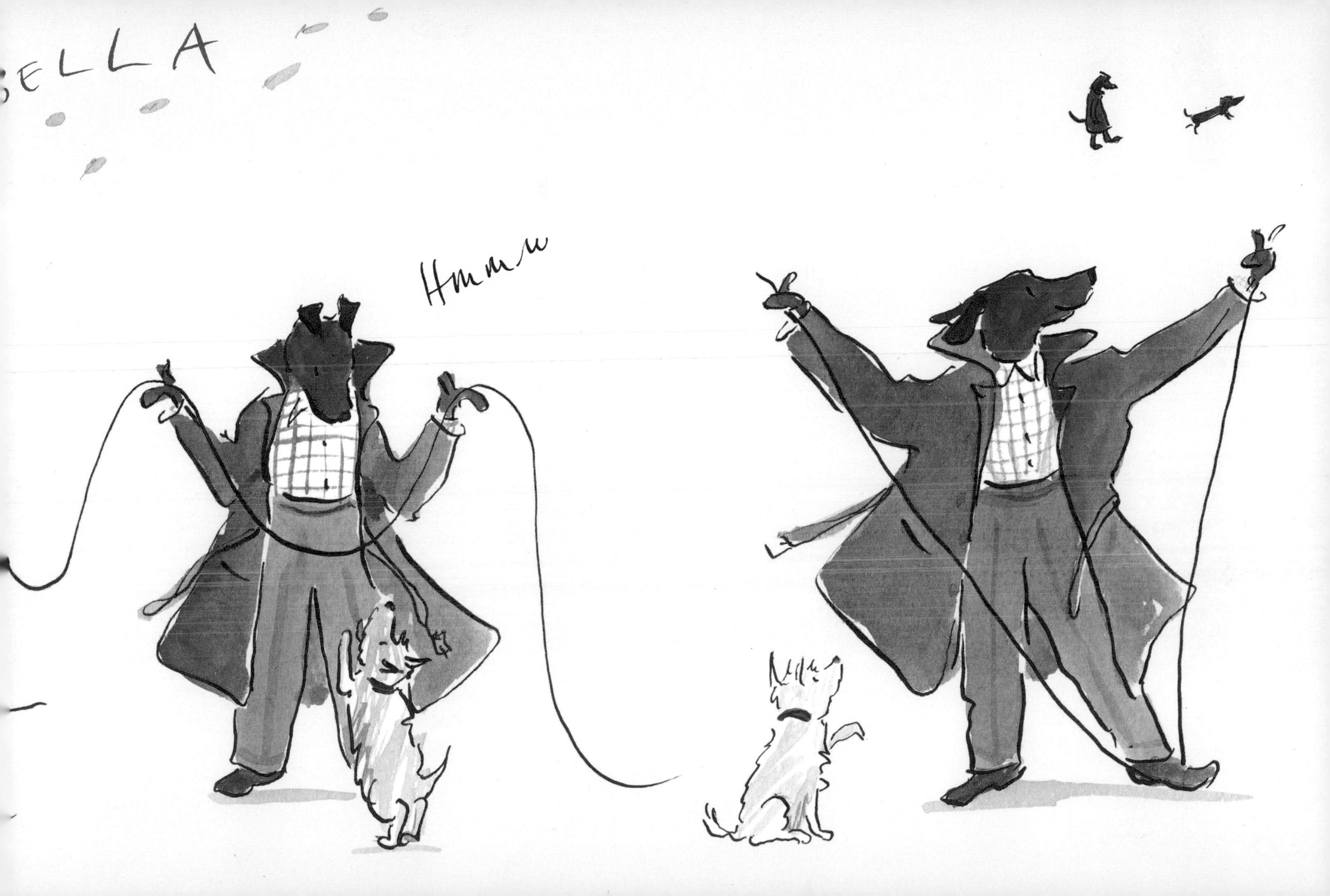
ELLA
Hmmm

BELLA

ONE!

TWO, THREE-FOUR-FIVE

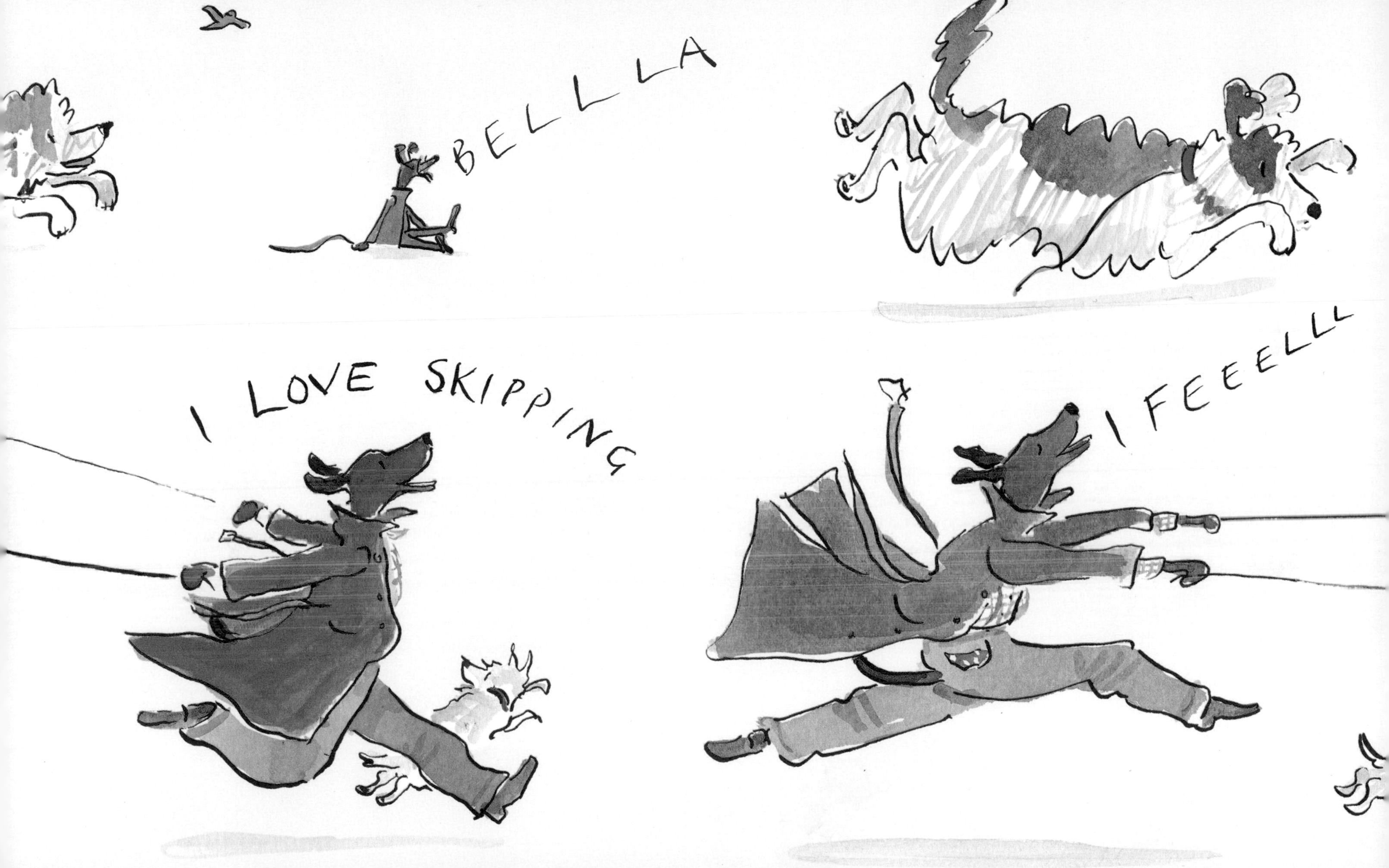
BELLLA
I LOVE SKIPPING
I FEEELLL

OH
NOOOOOOOOO

SQUASHED

OH, BELLA!
I'M SO SORRY... SHE'S VERY LOVING REALLY... FULL OF ENERGY... DOESN'T KNOW HER OWN STRENGTH...

"SHE LICKS PEOPLE... I JUST DON'T KNOW WHAT TO DO...
SHE DOESN'T KNOW HOW TO JOIN IN...
I'VE TRIED EVERYTHING...

FIVE HUNDRED

TWENTY THOUSAND

ONE MILLION TWENTY TRILLION AND THREE . . .
MUST NOT LOSE COUNT . . . MUST NOT LOSE COUNT
MUST NOT LOSE COUNT . . .
ZZZZZ

The next morning...

THANK YOU THANK YOU THANK
THANK YOU
THANK YOU
THANK YOU

?

WOOF
WOOF WOOF

?!